Margery Williams

The
Velveteen
Rabbit
or
How Toys Become Real

Illustrated by
Jean Chandler

Foreword by Corey Nash

Designed by Carlo DeLucia

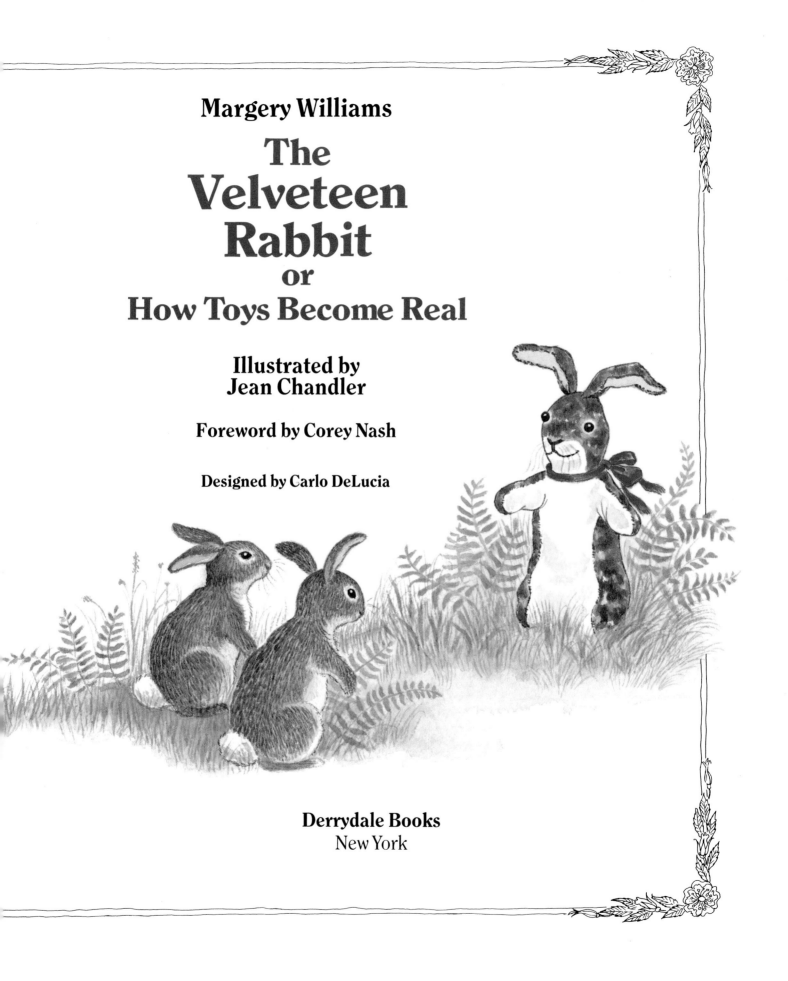

Derrydale Books
New York

To Francesco Bianco
from
The Velveteen Rabbit

This new edition first published in 1986 by Derrydale Books,
distributed by Crown Publishers, Inc., 225 Park Avenue South,
New York, New York 10003.

Printed and Bound in Japan.

Library of Congress Cataloging-in-Publication Data

Bianco, Margery Williams, 1880-1944.
    The velveteen rabbit, or, How toys become real.

Summary: By the time the velveteen rabbit is dirty, worn out, and about
to be burned, he has almost given up hope of ever finding the magic
called Real.
    [1. Toys—Fiction]   I. Title.   II. Title: How toys become real.
PZ8.9.B47Ve   1986   [Fic]   86—6347

ISBN 0-517-61813-3

h g f e d c b a

FOREWORD

The Velveteen Rabbit is a timeless story that can be enjoyed on many levels by readers of many ages. For it is more than just a simple tale for children.

It is the guileless story of a stuffed toy rabbit, once so well-loved and played with by the boy who owned him that he became shabby and his whiskers grew soft. Because the boy loved him, the rabbit was always beautiful to the boy; the boy needed him. And that was all that mattered to the rabbit. Nursery magic had made him Real to the boy. And when you are Real, shabbiness doesn't matter.

But it is also the story of an abandoned rabbit, forgotten and sad. And through the enchantment of the nursery magic fairy, he later became **REAL** to everyone.

To introduce this writer's interpretations of this wonderful tale would doubtless spoil it for first-time readers—and for those who return to this book again and again. Because on each rereading, a new story emerges.

This beautiful volume combines the enchanting classic text by Margery Williams with fanciful illustrations by Jean Chandler, especially created for this new edition. It is truly a book for the family to treasure and enjoy for generations.

Corey Nash

New York City
May 1986

There was once a velveteen rabbit, and in the beginning he was really splendid. He was fat and bunchy, as a rabbit should be; his coat was spotted brown and white, he had real thread whiskers, and his ears were lined with pink sateen. On Christmas morning, when he sat wedged in the top of the Boy's stocking, with a sprig of holly between his paws, the effect was charming.

There were other things in the stocking,
nuts and oranges and a toy engine, and
chocolate almonds and a clockwork mouse,
but the Rabbit was quite the best of all. For at
least two hours the Boy loved him, and then
Aunts and Uncles came to dinner, and there
was a great rustling of tissue paper and
unwrapping of parcels, and in the excitement
of looking at all the new presents the Velveteen
Rabbit was forgotten.

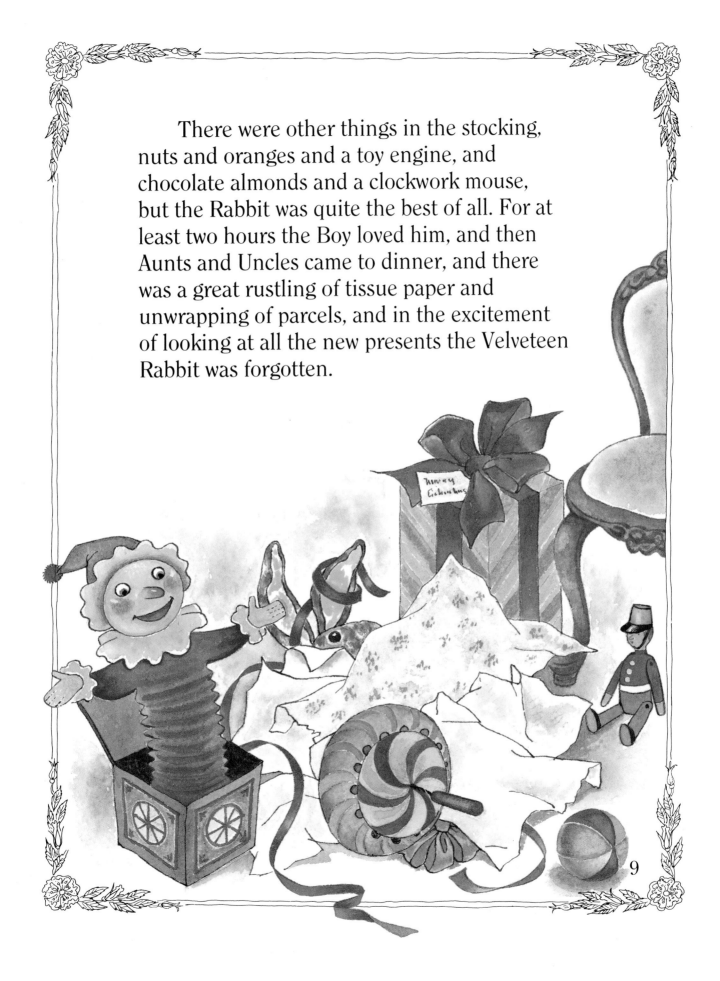

For a long time he lived in the toy cupboard or on the nursery floor, and no one thought very much about him. He was naturally shy, and being only made of velveteen, some of the more expensive toys quite snubbed him. The mechanical toys were very superior and looked down upon everyone else; they were full of modern ideas and pretended they were real. The model boat, who lived through two seasons and lost most of his paint, caught the tone from them and never missed an opportunity of referring to his rigging in technical terms. The Rabbit could not claim to be a model of anything, for he didn't know that real rabbits existed; he thought they were all stuffed with sawdust like himself, and he understood that sawdust was quite out-of-date and should never be mentioned in modern circles. Even Timothy, the jointed wooden lion, who was made by the disabled soldiers, and should have had broader views, put on airs and pretended he was connected with Government.

Between them all the poor little Rabbit was made to feel himself very insignificant and commonplace, and the only person who was kind to him at all was the Skin Horse.

The Skin Horse had lived longer in the nursery than any of the others. He was so old that his brown coat was bald in patches and showed the seams underneath, and most of the hairs in his tail had been pulled out to string bead necklaces. He was wise, for he had seen a long succession of mechanical toys arrive to boast and swagger, and by-and-by break their mainsprings and pass away, and he knew that they were only toys, and would never turn into anything else. For nursery magic is very strange and wonderful, and only those playthings that are old and wise and experienced like the Skin Horse understand all about it.

"What is Real?" asked the Rabbit one day, when they were lying side by side near the nursery fender, before Nana came to tidy the room. "Does it mean having things that buzz inside you and a stick-out handle?"

13

"Real isn't how you are made," said the Skin Horse. "It's a thing that happens to you. When a child loves you for a long, long time not just to play with, but *really* loves you, then you become Real."

"Does it hurt?" asked the Rabbit.

"Sometimes," said the Skin Horse, for he was always truthful. "When you are Real you don't mind being hurt."

"Does it happen all at once, like being wound up," he asked, "or bit by bit?"

"It doesn't happen all at once," said the Skin Horse. "You become. It takes a long time. That's why it doesn't often happen to people who break easily, or have sharp edges or who have to be carefully kept. Generally, by the time you are Real, most of your hair has been loved off, and your eyes drop out and you get loose in the joints and very shabby. But these things don't matter at all, because when you are Real you can't be ugly, except to people who don't understand."

"I suppose *you* are Real?" said the Rabbit. And then he wished he had not said it, for he thought the Skin Horse might be sensitive. But the Skin Horse only smiled.

"The Boy's Uncle made me Real," he said. "That was a great many years ago; but once you are Real you can't become unreal again. It lasts for always."

The Rabbit sighed. He thought it would be a long time before this magic called Real happened to him. He longed to become Real, to know what it felt like; and yet the idea of growing shabby and losing his eyes and whiskers was rather sad. He wished that he could become it without these uncomfortable things happening to him.

There was a person
called Nana who ruled
the nursery. Sometimes she
took no notice of the playthings
lying about, and sometimes, for no
reason whatever, she went swooping about
like a great wind and hustled them away in
cupboards. She called this "tidying up," and
the playthings all hated it, especially the tin
ones. The Rabbit didn't mind it so much, for
wherever he was thrown he came down soft.

One evening, when the Boy was going to
bed, he couldn't find the china dog that always
slept with him. Nana was in a hurry, and it was
too much trouble to hunt for china dogs at
bedtime, so she simply looked about her, and
seeing that the toy cupboard door stood open,
she made a swoop.

"Here," she said, "take your old Bunny! He'll do to sleep with you!" And she dragged the Rabbit out by one ear, and put him into the Boy's arms.

That night, and for many nights after, the
Velveteen Rabbit slept in the Boy's bed. At
first he found it rather uncomfortable, for the
Boy hugged him very tight, and sometimes he
rolled over on him, and sometimes he pushed
him so far under the pillow that the Rabbit
could scarcely breathe. And he missed, too,
those long moonlight hours in the nursery,
when all the house was silent, and his talks
with the Skin Horse. But very soon he grew
to like it, for the Boy used to talk to him,
and made nice tunnels for him under the

bedclothes that he said were like the burrows the real rabbits lived in. And they had splendid games together, in whispers, when Nana had gone away to her supper and left the nightlight burning on the mantelpiece. And when the Boy dropped off to sleep, the Rabbit would snuggle down close under his little warm chin and dream, with the Boy's hands clasped close round him all night long.

And so time went on, and the little Rabbit was very happy—so happy that he never noticed how his beautiful velveteen fur was getting shabbier and shabbier, and his tail coming unsewn, and all the pink rubbed off his nose where the Boy had kissed him.

19

Spring came, and they had long days
in the garden, for wherever the Boy went
the Rabbit went too. He had rides in the
wheelbarrow, and picnics on the grass, and
lovely fairy huts built for him under the
raspberry canes behind the flower border. And
once, when the Boy was called away suddenly
to go out to tea, the Rabbit was left out on the
lawn until long after dusk, and Nana had to
come and look for him with the candle because
the Boy couldn't go to sleep unless he was there.

He was wet through with the dew and
quite earthy from diving into the burrows the
Boy had made for him in the flower bed, and
Nana grumbled as she rubbed him off with a
corner of her apron.

"You must have your old Bunny!" she said.
"Fancy all that fuss for a toy!"

The Boy sat up in bed and stretched out
his hands.

"Give me my Bunny!" he said, "You mustn't
say that. He isn't a toy. He's *Real!*"

When the little Rabbit heard that, he was happy, for he knew that what the Skin Horse had said was true at last. The nursery magic had happened to him, and he was a toy no longer. He was Real. The Boy himself had said it.

That night he was almost too happy to sleep, and so much love stirred in his little sawdust heart that it almost burst. And into his boot-button eyes, that had long ago lost their polish, there came a look of wisdom and beauty, so that even Nana noticed it next morning when she picked him up, and said, "I declare if that old Bunny hasn't got quite a knowing expression!"

That was a wonderful Summer!

Near the house where they lived there was a wood, and in the long June evenings the Boy liked to go there after tea to play. He took the Velveteen Rabbit with him, and before he wandered off to pick flowers, or play at brigands among the trees, he always made the Rabbit a little nest somewhere among the bracken, where he would be quite cosy, for he was a kind-hearted little boy and he liked Bunny to be comfortable. One evening, while the Rabbit was lying there alone, watching the ants that ran to and fro between his velvet paws in the grass, he saw two strange beings creep out of the tall bracken near him.

They were rabbits like himself, but quite furry and brand new. They must have been very well made, for their seams didn't show at all, and they changed shape in a queer way when they moved; one minute they were long and thin and the next minute fat and bunchy, instead of always staying the same like he did. Their feet padded softly on the ground, and they crept quite close to him, twitching their noses, while the Rabbit stared hard to see which side the clockwork stuck out, for he knew that people who jump generally have something to wind them up. But he couldn't see it. They were evidently a new kind of rabbit altogether.

They stared at him, and the little Rabbit stared back. And all the time their noses twitched.

"Why don't you get up and play with us?" one of them asked.

"I don't feel like it," said the Rabbit, for he didn't want to explain that he had no clockwork.

"Ho!" said the furry rabbit. "It's as easy as anything." And he gave a big hop sideways and stood on his hind legs.

"I don't believe you can!" he said.

"I can!" said the little Rabbit. "I can jump higher than anything!" He meant when the Boy threw him, but of course he didn't want to say so.

"Can you hop on your hind legs?" asked the furry rabbit.

That was a dreadful question, for the Velveteen Rabbit had no hind legs at all! The back of him was made all in one piece, like a pincushion. He sat still in the bracken, and hoped that the other rabbits wouldn't notice.

"I don't want to!" he said again.

But the wild rabbits have very sharp eyes. And this one stretched out his neck and looked.

"He hasn't got any hind legs!" he called out. "Fancy a rabbit without any hind legs!" And he began to laugh.

"I have!" cried the little Rabbit. "I have got hind legs! I am sitting on them!"

"Then stretch them out and show me, like this!" said the wild rabbit. And he began to whirl round and dance, till the little Rabbit got quite dizzy.

"I don't like dancing," he said. "I'd rather sit still!"

But all the while he was longing to dance, for a funny new tickly feeling ran through him, and he felt he would give anything in the world to be able to jump about like these rabbits did.

The strange rabbit stopped dancing, and came quite close. He came so close this time that his long whiskers brushed the Velveteen Rabbit's ear, and then he wrinkled his nose suddenly and flattened his ears and jumped backwards.

"He doesn't smell right!" he exclaimed. "He isn't a rabbit at all! He isn't real!"

"I *am* Real!" said the little Rabbit. "I am Real! The Boy said so!" And he nearly began to cry.

Just then there was a sound of footsteps, and the Boy ran past near them, and with a stamp of feet and a flash of white tails the two strange rabbits disappeared.

"Come back and play with me!" called the little Rabbit. "Oh, do come back! I *know* I am Real!"

But there was no answer, only the little
ants ran to and fro, and the bracken swayed
gently where the two strangers had passed. The
Veveteen Rabbit was all alone.

"Oh, dear!" he thought. "Why did they run
away like that? Why couldn't they stop and talk
to me?"

For a long time he lay very still, watching
the bracken, and hoping that they would come
back. But they never returned, and presently
the sun sank lower and the little white moths
fluttered out, and the Boy came and carried
him home.

Weeks passed, and the little Rabbit grew very old and shabby, but the Boy loved him just as much. He loved him so hard that he loved all his whiskers off, and the pink lining to his ears turned gray, and his brown spots faded. He even began to lose his shape, and he scarcely looked like a rabbit anymore, except to the Boy. To him he was always beautiful, and that was all that the little Rabbit cared about. He didn't mind how he looked to other people, because the nursery magic had made him Real, and when you are Real, shabbiness doesn't matter.

And then, one day, the Boy was ill.

His face grew very flushed, and he talked in his sleep, and his little body was so hot that it burned the Rabbit when he held him close. Strange people came and went in the nursery, a light burned all night and through it all the little Velveteen Rabbit lay there, hidden from sight under the bedclothes, and he never stirred, for he was afraid that if they found him someone might take him away, and he knew that the Boy needed him.

It was a long weary time, for the Boy was too ill to play, and the little Rabbit found it rather dull with nothing to do all day long. But he snuggled down patiently, and looked forward to the time when the Boy should be well again, and they would go out in the garden among the flowers and the butterflies and play splendid games in the raspberry thicket like they used to. All sorts of delightful things he planned, and while the Boy lay half asleep he crept up close to the pillow and whispered them in his ear. And presently the fever turned, and the Boy got better. He was

33

able to sit up in bed and look at picture books, while the little Rabbit cuddled close at his side. And one day, they let him get up and dress.

It was a bright, sunny morning, and the windows stood wide open. They had carried the Boy out onto the balcony, wrapped in a shawl, and the little Rabbit lay tangled up among the bedclothes, thinking.

The Boy was going to the seaside tomorrow. Everything was arranged, and now it only remained to carry out the doctor's orders.

They talked about it all, while the little Rabbit
lay under the bedclothes, with just his head
peeping out, and listened. The room was to be
disinfected, and all the books and toys that the
Boy had played with in bed must be burned.

"Hurrah!" thought the little Rabbit.
"Tomorrow we shall go to the seaside!" For the
Boy had often talked of the seaside, and he
wanted very much to see the big waves coming
in, and the tiny crabs, and the sand castles.

Just then Nana caught sight of him.
"How about his old Bunny?" she asked.

"That?" said the doctor. "Why, it's a mass
of scarlet fever germs!—Burn it at once. What?
Nonsense! Get him a new one. He mustn't have
that anymore!"

And so the little Rabbit was put into a sack
with the old picture books and a lot of rubbish,
and carried out to the end of the garden
behind the fowl house. That was a fine place to
make a bonfire, only the gardener was too busy
just then to attend to it. He had the potatoes
to dig and the green peas to gather, but next
morning he promised to come quite early and
burn the whole lot.

That night the Boy slept in
a different bedroom, and
he had a new bunny to sleep
with him. It was a splendid
bunny, all white plush with
real glass eyes, but the Boy
was too excited to care
very much about it. For
tomorrow he was
going to the seaside,

and that in itself was such a wonderful thing that he could think of nothing else.

And while the Boy was asleep, dreaming of the seaside, the little Rabbit lay among the old picture books in the corner behind the fowl house, and he felt very lonely. The sack had been left untied, and so by wriggling a bit he was able to get his head through the opening and look out. He was shivering a little, for he had always been used to sleeping in a proper bed, and by this time his coat had worn so thin and threadbare from hugging that it was no longer any protection to him. Nearby he could see the thicket of raspberry canes, growing tall and close like a tropical jungle, in whose shadow he had played with the Boy on bygone mornings. He thought of those long sunlit hours in the garden—how happy they were—and a great sadness came over him. He seemed to see them all pass before him, each more beautiful than the other, the fairy huts in the flower bed, the quiet evenings in the wood when he lay in the bracken and the little ants ran over his paws; the wonderful day when he first knew that he was Real. He thought of the Skin Horse, so wise and gentle, and all that he had told him. Of what use was it to be loved and lose one's beauty and become Real if it all ended like this? And a tear, a real tear, trickled down his little shabby velvet nose and fell to the ground.

And then a strange thing happened. For where the tear had fallen a flower grew out of the ground, a mysterious flower, not at all like any that grew in the garden. It had slender green leaves the color of emeralds, and in the center of the leaves a blossom like a golden cup.

It was so beautiful that the little Rabbit
forgot to cry, and just lay there watching it. And
presently the blossom opened, and out of it
there stepped a fairy.

She was quite the loveliest fairy in the whole world. Her dress was of pearl and dewdrops, and there were flowers round her neck and in her hair, and her face was like the most perfect flower of all. And she came close to the little Rabbit and gathered him up in her arms and kissed him on his velveteen nose that was all damp from crying.

"Little Rabbit," she said, "don't you know who I am?"

The Rabbit looked up at her, and it seemed to him that he had seen her face before, but he couldn't think where.

"I am the nursery magic Fairy," she said.

"I take care of all the playthings that the children have loved. When they are old and worn out and the children don't need them anymore, then I come and take them away with me and turn them into Real."

"Wasn't I Real before?" asked the little Rabbit.

"You were Real to the Boy," the Fairy said, "because he loved you. Now you shall be Real to everyone."

41

And she held the little Rabbit close in her arms and flew with him into the wood.

It was light now, for the moon had risen. All the forest was beautiful, and the fronds of the bracken shone like frosted silver. In the open glade between the tree trunks the wild rabbits danced with their shadows on the velvet grass, but when they saw the Fairy they all stopped dancing and stood round in a ring to stare at her.

"I've brought you a new playfellow," the Fairy said. "You must be very kind to him and teach him all he needs to know in Rabbitland, for he is going to live with you forever and ever!"

And she kissed the little Rabbit again and put him down on the grass.

"Run and play, little Rabbit!" she said.

But the little Rabbit sat quite still for a moment and never moved. For when he saw all the wild rabbits dancing around him he

suddenly remembered about his hind legs, and
he didn't want them to see that he was made
all in one piece. He did not know that when
the Fairy kissed him that last time she had
changed him altogether. And he might have sat
there a long time, too shy to move, if just then
something hadn't tickled his nose, and before
he thought what he was doing he lifted his
hind toe to scratch it.

And he found that he actually had hind legs! Instead of dingy velveteen he had brown fur, soft and shiny, his ears twitched by themselves, and his whiskers were so long that they brushed the grass. He gave one leap and the joy of using those hind legs was so great that he went springing about the turf on them, jumping sideways and whirling round as the others did, and he grew so excited that when at last he did stop to look for the Fairy she had gone.

He was a Real Rabbit at last, at home with the other rabbits.

Autumn passed and Winter, and in the Spring, when the days grew warm and sunny, the Boy went out to play in the wood behind the house. And while he was playing, two rabbits crept out from the bracken and peeped at him. One of them was brown all over, but the other had strange markings under his fur, as though long ago he had been spotted, and the spots still showed through. And about his little soft nose and his round black eyes there was something familiar, so that the Boy thought to himself:

"Why, he looks just like my old Bunny that was lost when I had scarlet fever!"

But he never knew that it really was his own Bunny, come back to look at the child who had first helped him to be Real.